Val Priebe

illustrated by Tuesday Mourning

Librarian Reviewer
Chris Kreie, Media Specialist

Reading Consultant
Mary Evenson, Teacher

www.raintreepublishers.co.uk
Visit our website to find out
more information about
Raintree books.

To order:
☎ Phone 0845 6044371
🖨 Fax +44 (0) 1865 312263
💻 Email myorders@capstonepub.co.uk

Customers from outside the UK please telephone +44 1865 312262

Raintree is an imprint of Capstone Global Library Limited, a company incorporated in
England and Wales having its registered office at 7 Pilgrim Street, London, EC4V 6LB –
Registered company number: 6695582

"Raintree" is a registered trademark of Pearson Education Limited, under licence to
Capstone Global Library Limited

Text © Stone Arch Books 2009
First published by Stone Arch Books in 2009
First published in hardback and paperback in the United Kingdom by
Capstone Global Library in 2010
The moral rights of the proprietor have been asserted.

Edited in the United Kingdom by Diyan Leake
Original illustrations © Stone Arch Books 2009
Illustrated by Tuesday Mourning
Originated by Capstone Global Library Ltd
Printed in China by Leo Paper Products Ltd

ISBN 978 1 406 21384 3 (hardback)
14 13 12 11 10
10 9 8 7 6 5 4 3 2 1

ISBN 978 1 406 21405 5 (paperback)
14 13 12 11 10
10 9 8 7 6 5 4 3 2 1

British Library Cataloguing in Publication Data
Priebe, Val – Running rivals
A full catalogue record for this book is available from the British Library.

CONTENTS

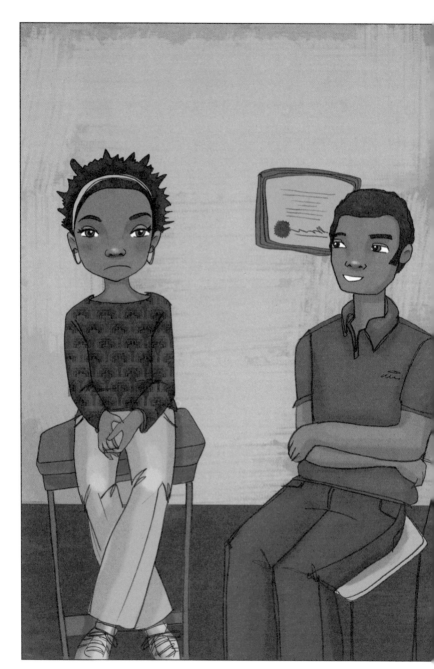

CHAPTER 1

BACK TO THE TEAM

The walls of Dr Smith's surgery were mint green. They were covered with certificates, diplomas, and drawings that looked like they'd been made by little kids.

My dad was sitting in a chair, reading a magazine. I was sitting on a stool, wishing that Dr Smith would hurry up.

All he had to do was walk in, look at my knee, and tell me whether it was healed enough for me to run again.

I was a mid-distance runner. I ran the 400. A lot of people think the 400 is the toughest track event. It's 400 metres, one lap around the track, running as fast as you can.

I usually came first. I came second if my biggest rival, Miranda Palmer, was running.

But you can't run at all if your knee has been hurt, like mine was. It had happened almost two months earlier, at the very beginning of the season.

There was a knock at the door and Dr Smith walked in. "Hi, Amy! Hi, Mr Reid! How are you two doing?" he asked.

Dr Smith shook my dad's hand. Then he got out an orange rubber hammer and started tapping on my knee.

"How has your knee been feeling?" he asked me.

"It feels normal," I told him. "Can I get back to my team?"

Dr Smith laughed. "That's why I love sports medicine," he said. "Athletes always want to get better so fast."

He looked at my chart and continued, "Well, I've looked at all of your X-rays and scans. Your knee seems to be healed. I'll let you go back, but you have to promise not to overdo it."

"I'll take it easy," I promised. "Anyway, we don't have a track meeting until Tuesday."

"Okay, Amy," the doctor said. "You'll have to start slowly, and make sure you're stretching and resting your knee after runs. Good luck on Tuesday." He shook my hand.

"Thanks, Dr Smith!" I said.

When we left the clinic, I was so excited that I jumped for joy. But my knee gave a little shake. I suddenly felt nervous.

What if my knee wasn't strong enough? What if I didn't have any speed?

The next meeting was only five days away. What if I wasn't ready?

CHAPTER 2
SCARED

"Wow, I didn't think he'd let you run again so soon," Dad said as we headed home. "Are you excited?"

"Yeah," I said. "Do we have an ice pack at home? I need to make sure to use it on my knee each time I've finished a run."

I was trying to change the subject. I didn't want to tell my dad how scared I was.

"Yes, we do. Hey, is everything okay?" asked Dad.

"Yes, fine," I replied.

"Good," said Dad. "Don't worry, honey. Tuesday's meeting will be here before you know it."

When we got home, I put my rucksack in my room, and then went into the dining room for dinner. For a few minutes, the only sounds were the clinks of forks and knives on plates.

"Natalie, how was school today?" asked my dad between bites.

"It was good," my older sister replied. "The yearbook is going really well."

"Great!" Dad said.

"Amy, what did the doctor say?" Natalie asked.

I felt my face turn red. I could hide my nervousness from my dad, but not from my sister. I looked down and answered, "I can go back to practice. Dr Smith said I had to be careful, though."

I concentrated really hard on cutting my chicken so I didn't have to look at her. Natalie could always tell if I wasn't telling her something by looking at my face.

"I think I'll go for a run after dinner," I said. I loved running. It always made me feel better. I guess it helped me think things through in my head.

"I found a new path in the park, and I don't have any homework," I added.

"Just don't push too hard," said Dad. "I'll have the ice pack ready for you when you get back."

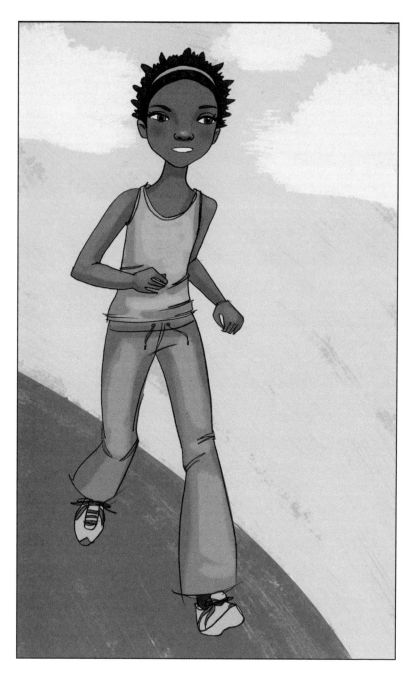

I went down the hall to my room and changed my clothes. I was really worried about my knee as I slipped out the back door. I walked across the street and into the park, stretching as I went.

When I got to the beginning of the path, I began to jog.

CHAPTER 3
A DIFFERENT TRACK

I usually ran on the track at school, but so did all of my teammates. I didn't want them to see me if I had to stop or if I was slow. I just wanted to run. So I headed to a different track from usual.

Concentrating on my breathing and form, I ran up a little hill. Just on the other side, the trees cleared and I could see a tennis court, two basketball hoops, and a track.

I started to jog down the hill towards the track. Then I noticed a flash of purple under the track lights.

It was a girl. She was tall and had a long brown ponytail. She was wearing purple and gold, the colours of our rival school, Five Acres.

I stopped and waited just out of sight. When the girl rounded a corner, I realized who she was. It was Miranda Palmer. Why was she running there?

Miranda was my biggest competition for the 400. She and I had been running against each other since Year 6, and she almost always beat me. And to make matters even worse, she'd been running next to me when I was hurt earlier in the season.

The meeting was at Five Acres. I had been in lane one, the closest to the inside of the track. Miranda had been in lane two. When the starting gun went off, I had burst out into the lead. From the corner of my eye, I could see that Miranda was keeping pace with me.

As we rounded the second turn, I had glanced over at Miranda.

That was the biggest mistake I could have made.

When I looked away, I stepped just a little too close to the edge of the track. My shoe got caught on the plastic between the grass and the asphalt.

I felt a pop, and then a lot of pain in my left knee.

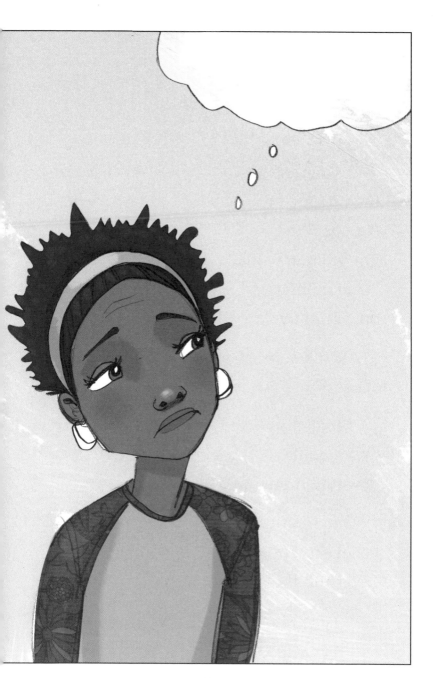

Somehow, I managed to finish the race. I came last. And then my dad took me to the hospital. I hadn't run since.

A woman's voice snapped me back to the present. "You had a good kick there at the end," the woman called to Miranda. The woman was standing just off the track. "One minute and five seconds," she went on. "That's your best time all year."

"Really?" said Miranda, panting slightly. "Great!"

"It's getting late," said the woman. "Why don't you jog a couple of laps to cool down, and then we'll go."

One minute and five seconds? I couldn't believe it. That was a great time. I had never run the 400 that fast.

"Okay, Mum," Miranda said.

I sat for a while. I just listened to Miranda's footsteps.

Her mum was right. It was getting late. As I turned to jog back up the hill, my knee gave another shake. My heart sank. Miranda was running a very fast 400 and I could hardly jog without pain.

Dad had the ice pack waiting for me when I got home. It was so cold I had to close my eyes and grit my teeth as I put it on to my knee.

Then Natalie walked in. "Hey, Amy. How was your run?" she asked.

"Fine," I said. I looked away.

"It wasn't fine," she said, frowning. "When you're ready to talk, you know where to find me."

CHAPTER 4

OUT OF PRACTICE

The next day was Friday. I was really looking forward to getting back to practice. It seemed like the school day lasted forever.

As soon I arrived at the sports field after school, I found Mr Meadows, my PE teacher.

"Amy! I'm so glad to have you back," said Mr Meadows. "How's your knee feeling?"

"It's okay," I said, looking away.

The truth was that my knee was sore from my run the night before. I didn't tell Mr Meadows. I didn't want him to worry.

"Are you ready for practice?" Mr Meadows asked.

"Absolutely," I said.

"Great," he said. Then he blew his whistle. "Okay, team," he called. "Let's do two laps and stretch." He blew his whistle again and we started running.

After we stretched, my knee was still sore, but not really painful. It seemed okay.

Then we split up. The people who did field events, like the discus or high jump, went to practise their throws and jumps. The long-distance runners took the three outside lanes of the track and started running.

Those of us who started our races with starting blocks (the 100-metre, 200-metre, and most of the 400-metre runners) each had a partner. The other person stood on the block so that it wouldn't move. Then, after the race started, they took the block off the track.

My partner was a girl named Katie. We grabbed a set of blocks. Katie said, "Amy, I'm so glad you're back. I've had to practise starting with Mr Meadows. He makes me so nervous!"

"Oh, Katie, that's too bad," I said with a laugh. "I'm glad to be back too. Is it okay if I go first?"

"Sure," said Katie.

I set up the blocks at the starting line and adjusted them.

Katie stood on the back of the blocks. I put my feet up against the blocks and got down on one knee. She waited as I lined my hands up to the starting line.

When my hands were in place, Katie said, "On your marks! Get set!"

I pushed up so that my knee was off the ground. But just before she yelled, "Go!" I shot out of the blocks and ran a few metres. That was a false start. In a real race, that would have disqualified me.

We tried a few more times, but I just kept false starting. I was so afraid of starting slow that I couldn't relax and wait.

"Don't worry about it, Amy. You're just out of practice," said Katie.

"Yeah, that's probably it," I said. "Your turn."

I got up. The starting position was making my knee sore anyway.

When Katie had finished practising her starts, we were rounded up with the rest of the runners. We were going to do an exercise called the Caterpillar.

We all ran in a line, one behind the other, around the track. Every so often, the last person in the line would sprint to the front.

It felt so good to be back, running next to my teammates. It was a beautiful, sunny day for my first practice back.

As we ran, I timed my breathing with my footsteps, in for two and out for two. I just listened to the sounds of our footsteps on the ground and let myself be happy to be back, running along the track.

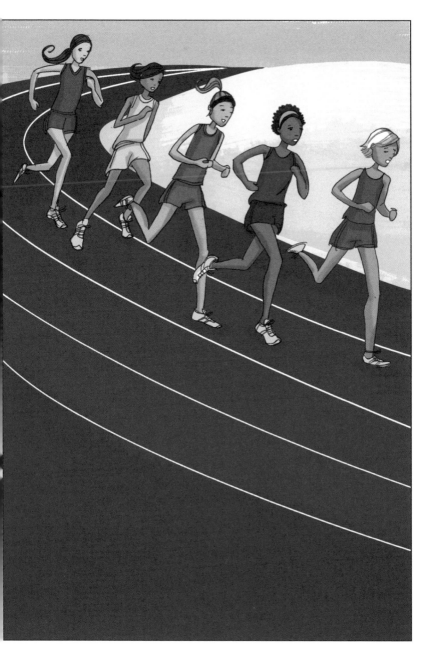

But the longer I ran, the more my knee hurt. I was glad when Mr Meadows finally blew his whistle.

"Great practice today, everyone," he said. "Now, you all know we have two meetings next week, on Tuesday and Friday. So get some rest this weekend and get ready for a big week. Have a great weekend!"

CHAPTER 5

NATALIE'S IDEA

I woke up late on Saturday morning. Natalie was in the kitchen when I went to find something to eat.

"Are you ready to tell me what's bothering you, Amy?" she asked. She looked at me over her glass of orange juice.

I knew she was trying to help me feel better. I just wasn't ready to talk about my fears.

"I'm fine, Natalie. Really," I said.

My sister raised her eyebrows. I could tell that she didn't believe me.

"What?" I asked her.

"Well," she said, "you haven't been able to talk about running lately without looking away from me. It's your favourite thing. Why are you acting like you don't like it anymore?"

"I do still like it!" I answered.

"Then what's the problem?" she asked again. "Amy, you know me. I'm not leaving you alone until you tell me."

Great, I thought. Natalie could be really stubborn when she wanted something.

"Okay," I said. "I had a hard time with starts yesterday. I'm sure I was just kind of out of practice, though, so now will you leave me alone?"

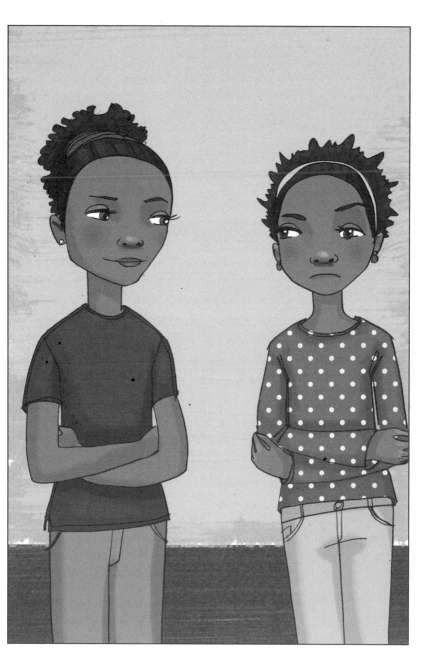

"Okay," said Natalie. "I need to have a shower and think for a bit. I'll come and find you when I'm done."

"You do that," I said under my breath. "I'm going for a run," I told her.

I wasn't normally so crabby with my sister, but the more I thought about the upcoming meetings, especially Friday's meeting against Miranda, the more scared I got. I didn't see how anyone could help me, so I just didn't want to talk about it at all.

* * *

When I got home, I was limping a little from the soreness in my knee and not feeling any better. I took some medicine to help my knee. When I came out of the bathroom, Natalie was waiting for me. She had a big smile on her face.

"Why are you so happy?" I asked, wiping my sweaty forehead with a towel.

"Because I had an idea," she replied. "What do you think about calling Mr Meadows and asking to use a set of blocks for the weekend?"

I stared at her. What did I think? "Natalie!" I shouted. "That's a great idea!"

CHAPTER 6

THE OLD AMY

I gave Natalie a sweaty hug while she screamed and tried to get away.

"I get it! I get it!" she cried, laughing. "You like the idea! Now get away from me and call Mr Meadows."

"Do you think he'll mind if I call him?" I asked nervously.

Natalie shook her head. "I doubt it," she told me. "He will be glad that you want to work hard over the weekend."

I grabbed the telephone. Mr Meadows answered on the second ring.

"Hello?" I said. "It's Amy."

"Good morning, Amy," said Mr Meadows. He sounded worried. "Is anything wrong? How's your knee?"

"It's fine, I'm fine," I said. I tried to ignore the nervous feeling in my stomach when he mentioned my knee. "I'm really sorry to call you at home, but I was hoping I could borrow a set of blocks for the weekend. Is that okay?"

"Oh! Sure!" Mr Meadows said. "That's a great idea!"

"It was Natalie's," I said honestly. I looked over to see her smiling at me. "Can you meet us at the school in twenty minutes?" I asked.

"Sure thing," he said. I gave Natalie a thumbs-up.

"Okay," I said. "See you then."

* * *

When we got home, Natalie and I planned our afternoon. She said, "I can hold your blocks for you. I was also thinking I could bang on a saucepan with a spoon for the starting gun."

I laughed. "We usually just say, 'Go,'" I told her, "but if you want to bang on a saucepan, you go right ahead."

Natalie blushed a little. "Right," she said. "I guess I got a little carried away." Then she laughed too.

We went into the garden and I did some stretches.

"Let's get you started," Natalie said when she had set up the blocks.

My first few attempts went as badly as they had at practice the day before. I false started every time. Every time, I was up and past the string we were using for a starting line before Natalie said go.

"Amy, just wait for it," she said after the fifth try, sounding frustrated. "It's not even a real race!"

"I know that, Natalie," I said, trying to be patient. "But you have to practise like it's the real thing."

Natalie sighed and stepped off the block. She put her hands on my shoulders. "Amy, I don't know what's really bothering you, but you're a good runner. You've worked so hard," she said.

Then she looked me in the eyes and said very slowly, "You can do this. I know you can. Just take a deep breath and try to relax."

The knot in my stomach, which had been getting worse with every start, loosened a little. I smiled at my sister.

Natalie and I worked until almost dinner time. My knee was sore by the time we finished, but not like it had been the day before. Towards the end, my old timing had started to come back. I was still a little bit too quick out of the blocks, but I felt more confident.

"That's better," said Natalie as we walked inside. "Almost like the old Amy."

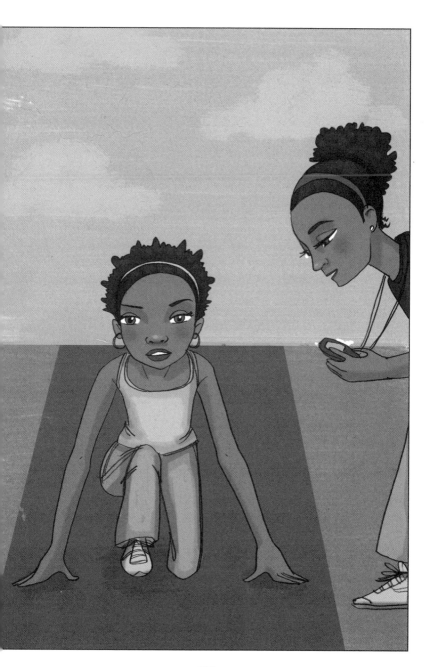

CHAPTER 7

THE FIRST MEETING

I was nervous about my first meeting, and Tuesday came fast. Miranda's school wasn't going to be at the meeting, though, so at least I could relax about that.

The meeting was at our school. After lessons ended, Katie and I took our time changing into our kit and making our way to the field.

"How are you feeling, Amy?" asked Katie as we changed. "Are you nervous?"

"A little," I said. "It'll be good to get this meeting over with so I can concentrate on Friday."

"Well," said Katie, "I'm really glad you're back."

I smiled and said, "Thanks, Katie. I'm really glad to be back. I can't believe how much I missed all this hard work!"

We laughed. Then we walked towards the team camp in the middle of the field.

Soon the meeting started. I jogged between starting lines, sand pits, finish lines, and jumps to cheer for my teammates. Race after race finished.

Finally, it was time to find out which lane I would run in. The official with the clipboard was a short, grey-haired lady with bright pink shoes.

"Name, please," she said, glancing at my shirt to see the name of my school.

"Amy Reid," I replied.

"You're in lane three today, Amy," said the official.

I walked over to the starting line and began to stretch.

A few minutes later, a voice called over the loudspeaker, "Last call for the girls' 400-metre run. All runners to the starting line!"

I found an out-of-the-way patch of grass and took off my tracksuit bottoms and hoodie. I had goosebumps on my arms and legs.

It was so cold out. I walked to lane three and hopped up and down, trying to keep warm.

An official yelled, "On your marks!"

I lowered myself to the asphalt. I pushed my right foot, then my left foot, up against the starting block.

"Get set!" yelled the official.

I tried to breathe, but I was so nervous and cold that it wasn't easy. I just kept telling myself to wait for the starting gun.

BANG!

The gun went off. I pushed myself as hard as I could out of the blocks.

After a few seconds, my left knee gave that familiar shake. I felt like I was running in slow motion.

All of the runners rounded the first turn close together. Then we headed into a straight stretch.

The runners in lanes two and six were ahead of me.

I was still in third place as we hit the second turn. My knee was tightening up with each stride.

There were less than a hundred metres to go. I fell back into fourth place.

Fifty metres to go.

I used all the strength I had. I passed the runner in lane one.

With twenty-five metres left, the girl in lane one passed me again. I could hear my teammates cheering me on.

I pushed myself as hard as I could for the last ten metres, passing the runner in lane six at the very end. I finished the race in third place.

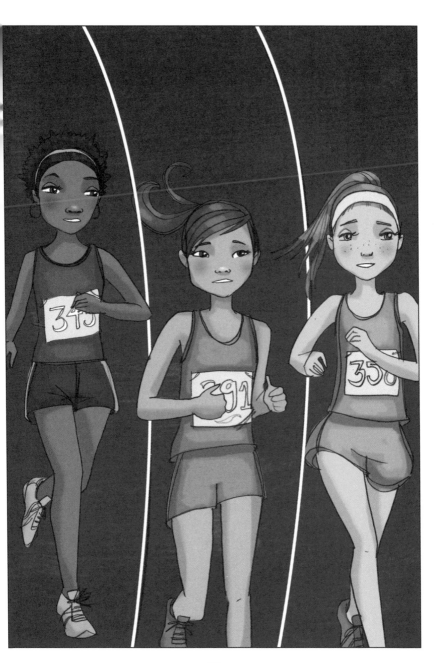

I was out of breath and hurting. Soon, Katie came running up with my jacket and tracksuit bottoms.

"Thanks, Katie," I said, grateful to be warm again. "What was my time?"

Katie looked away. "One minute and ten seconds, Amy," she said softly.

My jaw dropped. I had never run so slowly! One minute and ten seconds was only about four seconds slower than my normal time, but in a race as short as the 400, four seconds is like forever!

I bent down to untie my laces so that Katie wouldn't see the tears in my eyes. There was no way I would ever be ready to run against Miranda on Friday.

CHAPTER 8

ANOTHER IDEA

When I got home, I went straight into my room. I was hoping for some privacy, but my dad knocked on my door.

"Can I come in?" he asked.

"Why?" I asked. I wasn't in the mood to talk to anyone.

"I want to talk to you, honey. I want to make sure you're okay," he replied.

"All right," I said, sighing. "It's open."

Dad walked in. "Sweetie, will you come into the kitchen and talk to me?" he asked. He looked worried. I got up and followed him.

"What's going on?" he asked.

"I ran a one minute ten tonight," I said. "I have never run that slowly!" I wanted to cry again, and my voice shook a little.

"I know," my dad said. "But I feel like there's something else. You haven't been yourself since we got back from Dr Smith's surgery."

He put his hand on my head. "Tell your old dad what's on your mind." Dad looked at me. We were both quiet for a long time.

Finally, before I could change my mind, I told him everything.

I told him about my first thoughts of nervousness, about worrying about my knee, about seeing Miranda in the park, about my false starts, and finally, about my really huge fear that I wouldn't be ready for Friday's meeting. It was the final meeting of the year. It was a really big deal.

"Miranda has had two more months of practice than me," I finished. "She's been running faster than I've ever run. Today I tried as hard as I could and ran slower than ever."

Dad looked at me for a few seconds. He seemed to be thinking hard.

"Have you talked to Mr Meadows about any of this?" he asked finally.

"Dad, I haven't talked to anyone about any of this," I said.

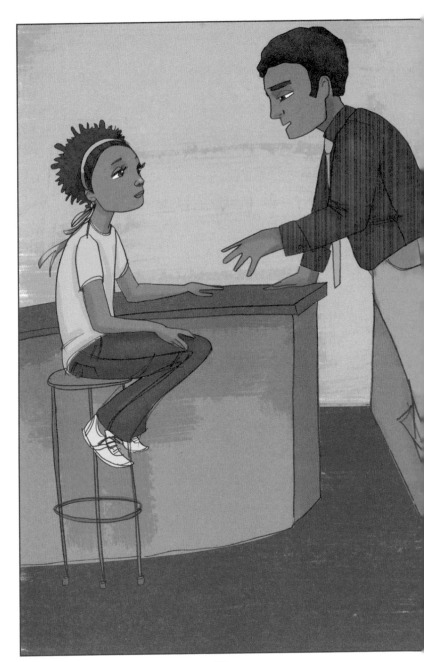

"Oh, honey. I don't know what to tell you," Dad said with a sigh. "All you can do is your best. And you still have Friday's meeting, right? I'm sure your slow run tonight was just you being nervous. Plus, you're still getting back into shape."

"Yeah," I said.

My dad didn't seem to understand how upset I was. I needed to talk to Natalie. My sister was always really good at solving problems.

"Dad?" I asked. "I need to talk to Natalie," I said. "No offence or anything," I added quickly.

"I understand, Amy. I'll go and get her for you." Dad said as he stood up. He even looked a little relieved.

Soon, my sister walked into the kitchen.

"Okay, Amy," Natalie said, sitting down next to me. "Dad told me everything, and I have an idea."

She took a deep breath. Then she went on, "Why don't you go to the track in the park and talk to Miranda? Maybe you can practise with her or something."

That wasn't exactly what I had in mind. "You must be joking," I said.

"No, I'm not. She's just a girl who likes to run, like you are," said Natalie.

I sat for a few seconds to let the idea sink in. "Will you come with me?" I asked finally.

"Yeah," she said. Then she smiled. "I'm not running, though."

I laughed. "Deal," I said. "We'll go tomorrow after dinner."

CHAPTER 9

MY BIGGEST COMPETITION

The next day, Natalie picked me up after practice. "Are you ready for tonight?" she asked.

"No," I said.

"Amy!" exclaimed Natalie. "We talked about this yesterday. Did you change your mind?"

"No," I said again. "Miranda just makes me really nervous. She always wins."

"I bet she's just as impressed by you," said Natalie.

But I didn't think so.

* * *

After dinner, I put on my running clothes. Ten minutes later, Natalie and I were heading for the track.

As soon as we reached the track, I saw Miranda. She was sprinting through the last hundred metres of a lap.

I started to turn around, but Natalie held on to my elbow and guided me towards the track.

Miranda stopped running as we walked up. She squinted at us through the fence. "Amy Reid? Is that you?" she asked.

"Yeah," I said, surprised. "How do you know my name?"

Miranda laughed. "Because you're my biggest competition!" she said. "What are you doing here?"

"Well, I live near here," I told her. "This is my sister, Natalie." Natalie and Miranda smiled at each other.

I took a deep breath and went on, "So anyway, I was running near the track last week and saw you practising." I looked at my sister for help.

"Amy had a rough meeting last night. I suggested she come to ask you for some advice," Natalie said. "I mean, I know you're on different teams and everything, but . . ." She stopped. Miranda had started to blush.

"Are you kidding?" asked Miranda. "I should ask Amy for advice!"

I was shocked. "About what?" I asked.

"Your form!" Miranda said. "Your form is always so perfect."

Then Natalie said, "If you two are going to practise, you should really get started."

Miranda and I went to the starting line. We decided to run the first lap in our own styles, so that we could see the differences side-by-side.

We were really close for the first half, but I was in the lead.

I noticed that Miranda's elbows seemed to fly out from her body a little. It was almost as if she was having trouble keeping her arms in close like you're supposed to.

We went around the second turn. That's when Miranda sped up.

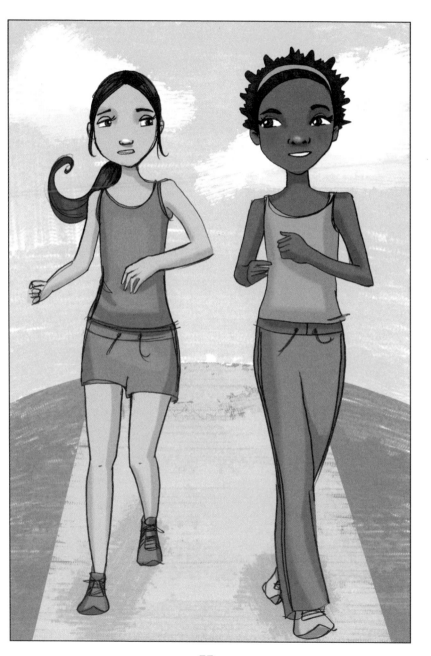

I tried to keep up with her, but I was out of energy. Plus, my knee was bothering me again.

Miranda beat me by about two metres. That's a lot in such a short race.

After we caught our breath, I asked, "What's your secret?"

"I used to try to sprint the whole thing, but I was always so wiped out by the end. My PE teacher suggested I try it a different way," Miranda explained. "If you run a little slower than normal for the first half of the race, you can speed up for the second half and pass everyone." She shrugged. "It works really well."

I thought for a minute. "Okay," I said. "Let's run it again. This time I'll try it your way."

We ran another lap. That time, I actually beat her!

After we cooled down a little, I gave Miranda some tips on keeping her elbows in close to her body. "I just pretend I'm on one of those ski machines, you know?" I told her. "Like on TV? It takes some getting used to, but keeping your elbows in really makes a difference."

Finally, I noticed that the sun was below the trees, so we decided to call it a night.

"See you on Friday!" called Miranda as Natalie and I headed back down the trail towards home.

"See you then!" I yelled back.

I felt happier than I had in days.

CHAPTER 10

PERSONAL BEST

Friday morning was chilly and sunny. But by the time we changed and boarded the bus to drive to the meeting, the sky had clouded over, the wind had picked up, and the rain was coming down in sheets.

It was the worst possible weather for a track meeting. All of my good feelings from Wednesday night disappeared.

The drive to Five Acres didn't take long, but it felt like forever.

The rain had let up a little by the time we got there, but the wind was still blowing. To make matters worse, it seemed like the rain and cold were making my knee stiff.

I was sitting with Katie when Mr Meadows walked back and sat down in front of us. "Amy, how's your knee feeling?" he asked. "Because if anything could hurt your knee again, it would be running in this weather. So if you don't want to run today, you don't have to."

He saw the look on my face and quickly added, "But if you want to run, I think you should stay on the bus where it's warm and dry until it's your turn."

Soon, we arrived at the school. Little butterflies started to form in my stomach. I was so nervous.

This meeting was really important. Anyone who finished first or second in their event would compete in the Interschool Finals.

Usually, I'd have run in many meetings before this point in the season. But this season, I'd been out of action for two months. The finals at the end of the season had really sneaked up on me.

The time seemed to fly by as I waited for my race. Soon, Mr Meadows was telling me what lane I was going to run in. Then he led me off the bus.

I was in lane one. It was the same lane of the same track I had been hurt on.

I took my position in the lane. Miranda was right next to me, in lane two. We smiled at each other.

"On your marks!"

I crouched down and faced forwards.

"Get set!"

I pushed my toe as close as I could to the starting line without actually touching it.

BANG! The starting gun went off.

I concentrated all of my thoughts and effort on keeping up with Miranda.

When we hit the second curve, Miranda put on a burst of speed. I was surprised to find myself right next to her.

I was using Miranda's method for running. So far, it was making a big difference. We were neck and neck. My knee hurt a little, but I ignored it. Then Miranda pulled ahead. I pulled ahead of her for a few metres, but I couldn't keep my lead.

Suddenly, it was over. Miranda had won.

For a second, I felt really disappointed. Yet again, Miranda Palmer had beaten me.

But then Katie came running over. "Amy!" she called, sounding excited. "You ran it in one minute and five seconds!"

"Are you serious?" I asked. I felt shocked. That was my fastest time ever. "Did I really?" I couldn't believe it. How had I run in one minute and five seconds with a healing knee?

"Yeah, you really did," a girl's voice said.

I turned around. It was Miranda. "Congratulations," I told her. "You were great."

Miranda smiled. "You were too! Personal best, right? Your best time ever?" she asked. "That must feel great!"

I smiled back. "Yes, it was," I admitted. "It feels pretty good."

Miranda laughed. "Wait till the next meeting," she said.

"*You* wait till the next meeting," I joked. "Then my knee will be totally healed, and I'll be some serious competition!"

Everyone cheered as the official read our times into a microphone. I could see my dad and Natalie in the stands, jumping up and down.

"You already are serious competition," Miranda said, smiling. "I can't wait till the next meeting."

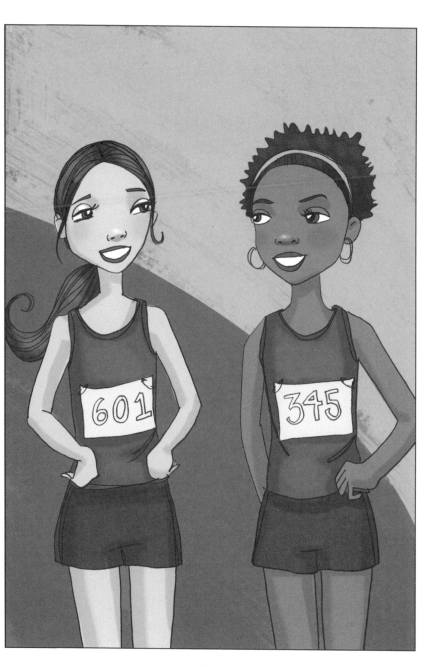

ABOUT THE AUTHOR

Val Priebe lives with her two crazy dogs, Bruce and Lily. Besides writing books, she loves to spend her time reading, knitting, cooking, and coaching basketball. Other books that Val has written in this series include *Full Court Dreams* and *Stolen Bases*.

ABOUT THE ILLUSTRATOR

When Tuesday Mourning was a little girl, she knew she wanted to be an artist when she grew up. Now, she is an illustrator who is especially keen on working on books for children and teenagers. When she isn't illustrating, Tuesday loves spending time with her husband, who is an actor, and their son, Atticus.

GLOSSARY

competition   person you are competing against

concentrate   focus your thoughts and attention on something

disqualified   prevented from taking part because of breaking a rule

form   the way a runner holds her body

lane   one of the strips a track is divided into

official   person who enforces the rules

pace   rate of speed

rival   person you are competing against

sprint   run fast over a short distance

GREAT FEMALE ATHLETES

Find out about female athletes who have reached the highest levels in their sport.

Kelly Homes

800- and 1500-metres runner

www.doublegold.co.uk

Paula Radcliffe

marathon runner

www.paularadcliffe.com

Sally Gunnell

hurdler

www.britisholympians.com

www.sallygunnell.com

Cathy Freeman

400-metre runner

http://en.wikipedia/wiki/Cathy-Freeman

www.olympic.org/uk/athletes/profiles/

bio_uk_asp?PAR_I_ID=69981

Shelly-Ann Fraser

100-metre sprinter

http://news.bbc.co.uk/sport1/hi/olympics/

athletics/7566834.stm

DISCUSSION QUESTIONS

1. Why did Amy want Natalie to help her get over her fear instead of her dad?

2. Why was Amy feeling nervous about being back on the track team?

3. Natalie tells Amy to try practising with Miranda. Would you practise with your rival? Talk about your answer.

WRITING PROMPTS

1. Have you ever been injured while playing a sport? Write about what happened.

2. Sometimes it can be interesting to think about a story from another character's point of view. Try writing chapter 10 from Miranda's point of view. What does she see and hear? How does she feel? What does she think about?

3. In this book, Amy asks her sister for help. Write about a time when you asked someone for help, even though you were embarrassed.

FIND OUT MORE

Books

Athletics **(Inside Sport series)**, Clive Gifford (Wayland, 2010)

Athletics **(Starting Sport series)**, Rebecca Hunter (Franklin Watts, 2009)

Track Athletics, Jason Page (Ticktock (Media, 2008)

Track Athletics **(Training to Succeed series)**, Rita Storey (Franklin Watts, 2009)

Websites

news.bbc.co.uk/sport1/hi/athletics/default.stm
This website will keep you up to date with athletics news from around the world.

www.uka.org.uk/e-inspire/hall-of-fame-athletes
Find out all about the greatest athletes in history on this website.